A Storm of Strawberries

Jo Cotterill

Piccadilly
PRESS

First published in Great Britain in 2017 by
PICCADILLY PRESS
80–81 Wimpole St, London W1G 9RE
www.piccadillypress.co.uk

Text copyright © Jo Cotterill, 2017

All rights reserved.
No part of this publication may be reproduced, stored or transmitted
in any form by any means, electronic, mechanical, photocopying or
otherwise, without the prior written permission of the publisher.

The right of Jo Cotterill to be identified as author of
this work has been asserted by her in accordance with the Copyright,
Designs and Patents Act, 1988

This is a work of fiction. Names, places, events and
incidents are either the products of the author's imagination
or used fictitiously. Any resemblance to actual persons,
living or dead, is purely coincidental.

A CIP catalogue record for this book is available
from the British Library.

ISBN: 978-1-84812-616-9
also available as an ebook

1

Typeset in Sabon 12/17.5pt by Palimpsest Book Production Limited,
Falkirk, Stirlingshire

Printed and bound by Clays Ltd, St Ives Plc

Piccadilly Press is an imprint of Bonnier Zaffre Ltd,
a Bonnier Publishing company
www.bonnierpublishing.com